Puss in Boots

Puss in Boots

RETOLD AND ILLUSTRATED BY
GAIL E. HALEY

DUTTON CHILDREN'S BOOKS

NEW YORK

Library of Congress Cataloging-in-Publication Data

Haley, Gail E.

  Puss in Boots / by Gail E. Haley.

     p.   cm.

  Summary: A cunning cat wins for his master a castle, a fortune, and the hand of a princess.

  ISBN 0-525-44740-7

  [1. Fairy tales. 2. Folklore—France.] I. Title.

PZ8.H135Pu

398.2—dc20

[E]   90-20629 CIP AC

Published in the United States by Dutton Children's Books,
a division of Penguin Books USA Inc.

Designer: Joseph Rutt

Printed in Hong Kong by South China Printing Co.

First Edition   10 9 8 7 6 5 4 3 2 1

For Clarence—veteran of two books, poet, head of the Kitty Committee: Pyewacket, Mata Hari, Esmerelda, Jet-Fidget, Gypsy Rover—and for Magic, Mittens, and Fairmont.

In loving memory of Woody Yellow Fellow, wherever you are, Woody Two-Shoes, Cleo, Skittles, Buster I, Buster II, Starbright, and all the catkind who still have a face, a name, and a home in my heart.

On the day the Miller was buried, his will was read. To his oldest son he bequeathed his mill. His second son received the donkey. To his youngest son Michael, he left only Grey, his cat.

Michael was dismayed. "My two brothers can join forces and earn a decent living," he thought to himself. "I am left without a home or anything except this useless cat."

As they left the mill, Michael regarded Grey. "What good are you to me out in the world? I might as well eat you and make a muff from your fur."

"Do not despair, Master," spoke the cat. "For I am not what I seem."

Michael was dumbfounded. He had never heard a cat speak! Shocked as he was, he listened to Grey, who had more to say.

"Give me a pair of boots and a good sack," the cat continued, "and you may yet have all that you dream."

Michael was very surprised to hear this request. But he
agreed immediately, for he had little to lose. Using his small
store of funds, he had a fine pair of boots and a sack made by
the village cobbler.

Grey looked tall and grand in his new boots. People from the
other shops gathered around to admire the splendid Puss in Boots.

Puss set off immediately with the sack slung over his
shoulder. He headed toward a field where rabbits were often
to be seen. Propping the sack open with a stick, he placed
some tender carrots inside. Then he lay down beside it,
pretending to be asleep, but kept the drawstring tight in his paw.

It was not long before a hapless young rabbit smelled the
bait and hopped inside the sack. Puss quickly pulled the
drawstring, and the rabbit was caught.

Pausing only to straighten his whiskers, Puss picked up the sack and set out at once for the King's palace. The elegant cat was admitted to the King's audience.

"Your Majesty," said Puss, bowing low, "I bring you this splendid young hare from my master, the Marquis of Carrabas."

The King could not recall the Marquis of Carrabas (for Puss had just made up the title), but he was amused. "Return my thanks to the Marquis, Master Puss in Boots," the King said.

The next day, Puss brought the King a brace of partridges and was rewarded with a small sack of gold coins. Michael was glad to receive the money, for now he and Puss could find bed and board.

In the days following, Puss took the King more game for his table. On one visit, the King surprised him with a magnificent plumed hat and a sword befitting a royal messenger, which Puss put on and wore thereafter.

On another visit, Puss learned from a friend inside the palace that the King and his daughter, Theresa, planned to go on a picnic in the country. Puss consulted his map to make sure he knew the exact route they would take, and he formed a clever plan.

Puss hurried back to his master and said, "Do exactly as I tell you, and your fortune is made." He led Michael to a bridge where the King's coach would cross a small river.

"Take off all your clothes and bathe in the river," said the cat. Michael did as he was told, and Puss threw away the ragged clothes.

As the King's coach approached the bridge, Puss stood up on the bridge and shouted, "Help! Help! My master, the Marquis of Carrabas, has been robbed!"

"Stop the carriage," ordered the King. "I know that cat!"

The King alighted from the carriage. He and his escorts called to Michael from the bank. "My dear fellow, what kind of disaster has befallen you?"

"While I was swimming, your Majesty," said Michael, "two stout fellows stole my clothes and arms and made off with them."

"Fetch some clothes for the Marquis at once," ordered the King.

A fine suit was brought for Michael, and when he put it on, he was as grand as anyone in the King's court.

He was introduced to the King's daughter, Theresa, who thought him quite handsome. She was delighted that he was the companion of the elegant cat she had seen at court. Her own cat, Letitia, slept under her arm every night.

The King invited Michael and his cat to join them on the picnic, but Puss declined. He had important errands to attend to.

Puss hurried on till he came to a vast field where peasants toiled at harvesting grain.

"The King is coming," shouted Puss, drawing his sword. "Tell him that this field belongs to the Marquis of Carrabas, or I shall cut you to ribbons." Then he added more kindly, "If you do as I say, I will come back and give you a fine reward."

The surrounding countryside really belonged to Moustaphus, the Many-Faced. He was a vain ogre and was also known as a Shape Changer. Puss then headed for the ogre's palace across the fields, informing all the peasants he met of what they were to say.

The ogre, who did not receive
many visitors, welcomed Puss.

"Greetings, Puss in Boots," he
snarled. "What brings such a grand
fellow into my dreadful presence?"

"Oh Great and Terrible
Wizardness," said Puss, "I have
journeyed far to find you. For it is
said abroad that you can change your
shape into anything you like. I have
come to see this wonder for myself,
even if it should cost me my life."

Moustaphus, of course, was greatly
flattered by Puss's admiration.

And so, as quick as lightning, the ogre changed himself into a raging lion. "Is this my true shape, Master Puss in Boots," he roared, "or do you think it is some other?"

"That's very impressive, your Ogreness," said Puss, "but I am not surprised to see you become large and fierce. You are fierce most of the time. I don't suppose it would be *possible* for you to change yourself into something small and defenseless …something as small as a mouse, perhaps?"

"DONE!" roared the ogre.
"Is this *small enough?*" squeaked
Moustaphus the mouse.

"Most adequate," replied Puss,
who leaped upon him and gobbled
him up in an instant.

His meal done, Puss surveyed the
palace. From a window he could see
the royal party approaching.

As the King passed through the ogre's fields, he was told by the peasants that the land belonged to the Marquis of Carrabas. The King was much impressed.

Puss waited at the gates of the palace. "Welcome to the home of my master," Puss announced happily.

Puss showed the royal party through the palace with its ballroom, magnificent furniture, exotic gardens, and treasury. The King was soon convinced that the Marquis must be one of the wealthiest men in his kingdom.

On their long ride through the countryside, Michael and Theresa had fallen deeply in love. So the new Marquis lost no time in asking for the hand of the Princess.

The King happily gave his consent. And when it was discovered that Grey and Letitia, the Princess's cat, were also in love, it became a double wedding. The week-long ceremony was the most splendid that the court had ever seen.

Michael and Theresa enjoyed the rule of their happy
kingdom until the end of their days. They had many
children and grandchildren.

And so did Puss in Boots—the Master Cat.

FOOTNOTES

The old King was so pleased with the birth of his first grandchild that he created The Paw Law: All cats in the land have a right to food and a place by the fire, with tickles whenever needed.

The Master Cat, true to his promise to the peasants, asked the Marquis to decree that henceforth all people had a right to share in the profits of their labors. Michael, knowing what it was like to be poor, granted his wish immediately.